#1

ELERFINE

Written and Illustrated by Neal Hopkin

A Note for The Reader:
Language is critical in this volume of Elerfine.
When you see this font, the character is speaking in goblin.
when you see this font, the character is speaking in the common language.

My Personal Thanks:
I have shamelessly dedicated this book to myself! 2020 was a rough
year for most, as it certainly was for me. I needed something to work on
that was all my own, and this comic was that something. It is the first
comic I've ever created, and it took all of 2020 to finish. I poured a lot of
work into it, and I hope it brings you a portion of the joy it gave me.
Thank you for your support and interest. And thanks to my big brother
and GM Luke Hopkin for the story inspiration.

I'll be doing a lot more with comics, so please
visit **Elerfine.com** to follow along.

Volume #2 is already in the works.
The story continues at Elerfine.com

Urgla-ak talt urgla-ak, hehe.
(Poke poke fun, poke poke, hehe.)

Urgla-ak talt, trax-rac!
(Poke poke fun, my turn!)

No Wrorx, use stick for poke poke.

Wrorx warrrior, not runt, Wrorx's blade thirsty.

Black-Hand order me guard elf prisoner! You want disobey Black Hand?

There, poke poke the human prisoner there!

NO! WAIT DON'T

UNNGH!

Urgla-ak talt..
Hehehe

Why do you always protect me, Frank? I'm smart enough to know the Black-Hand gave no such order.

Then you're also smart enough to know I do this for my own gain.

To be oblivious means to be unaware or merely not concerned with what is happening. I would say that goblins fit either - or even both - of those descriptions.

But then... here you are concerned about me.

Yes... here am I.

North Elerfine Forest

This is the site I was telling you about. There used to be a red barn here.

And you think the goblins dismantled it for some purpose?

That's what our intel suggests.

As soon as Rhykos is done with his prayers, we'll go find out for sure.

Bahamut, grant me power to mercilessly eradicate this evil filth from the land.

Blood shall drench the earth in your mighty name this day.

We won't have any difficulty tracking them, they've left plenty of footprints.

No need to track the goblins, Varis. I can smell their evil from here.

Oh look, Rhykos is finally done. We can all be on our way now.

Ladies first Seldein.

Thank You, Kurn.

C'mon Thuas, evil is afoot!

Thyren and I are right behind you Rhykos.

Frank, do you remember the day you asked me to teach you? It's like you had an awakening of the mind. You were different than before. You had curious eyes. What happened that day?

I DO remember Raspen.

Nothing special happened. I found a parchment while out hunting. I'd seen writing before, but I'd never wondered what it meant. It was so small, I figured I must be able to understand such a small thing.

I squinted real hard at it, but nothing happened. I thought that squinting might be all it took. HA! I had no concept of what reading really was. So dumb, but I did have one good idea that day, to bring the sheet to you, so that's what I did.

And that was all? Nobody cast a spell on you? You didn't touch some magic relic?

I think I'd have remembered that, but I was so incredibly oblivious back then.

And it only turned out to be some human's market list.

You grunted some goblin words at me and pointed to the letters. The rest is history.

It took about 8 months, but I was determined and you were a great teacher.

And why the determination?

I felt... something new. Something I don't think any goblin ever felt-- my own ignorance.

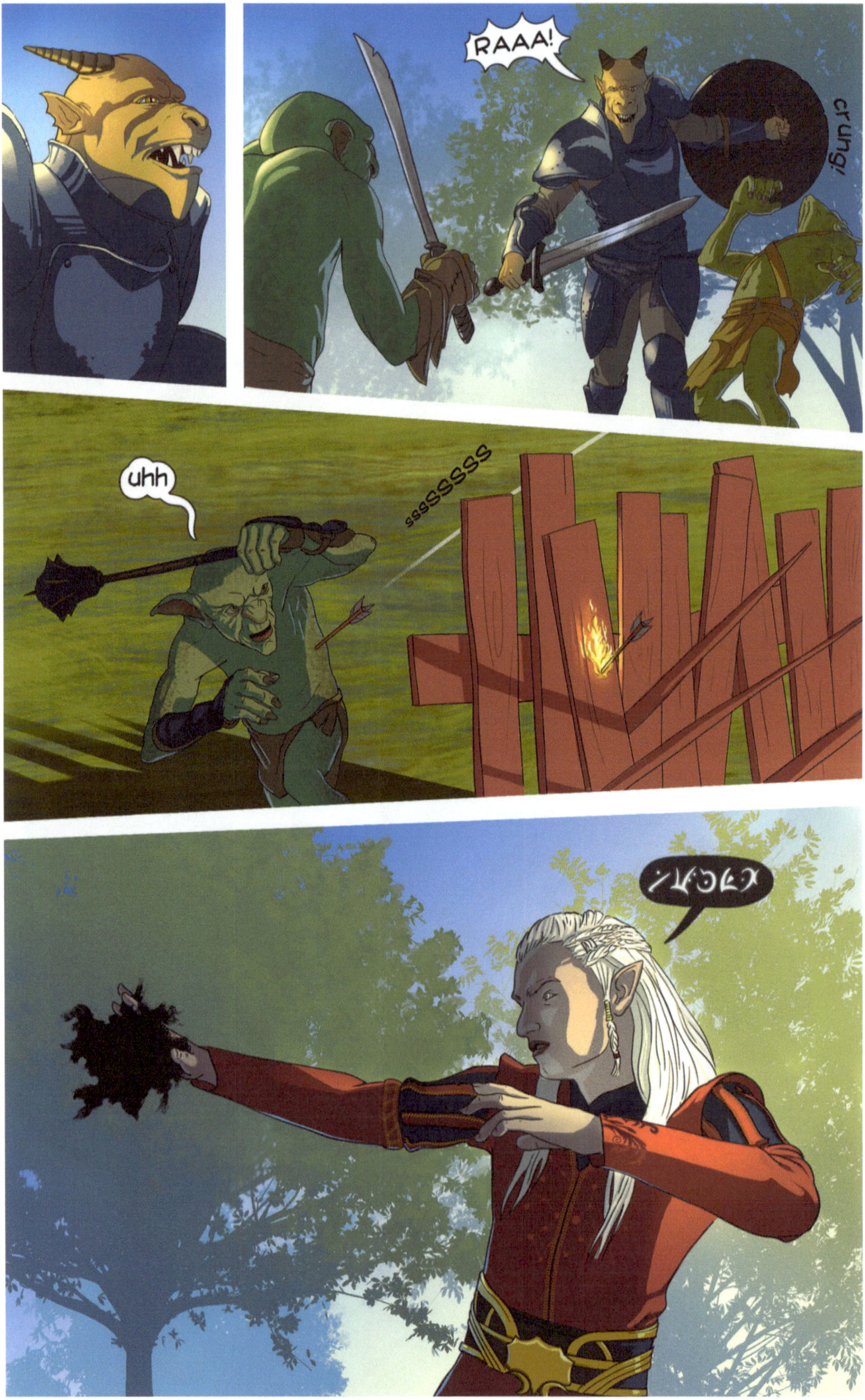
RAAA!
crung!
uhh
sssSSSSSS

Respen, I brought you another book. The other goblins just toss books out!

Great, something to pass the time. If these cells hadn't been built by ancient dwarves, I'd have been out of here many seasons ago.

THE IGNORANCE OF KING ULVIN

Ignorant is a fitting word for us. Goblins do horrible things, I did horrible things, but I don't believe we are inherently terrible creatures. We don't know any better.

We have a lot of mouths to feed. Goblins breed rampantly and without restraint. It's how we've managed to survive.

Other races farm and trade, but Goblins know nothing of these things. Now we've outgrown our lairs and must take up shelter in exposed ruins.

We've over-hunted this forest too. Desperation has driven us to desperate measures. Does this make us evil? Can we change our ways?

There is some order now, thanks to the Black-Hand.

He was the first to bring all the tribes together.
If there is another intelligent Goblin, it would be him.

Kulkta Akak Taltuk!

Hukla Sakt Kulkta!
Huh? Are you saying something? VARIS? You speak Goblin? This one really seems to want to...
Eh, what's the point ... Rrrra!

I am Rahl. This is Melroc. We have come to select the three best warriors among you to enter the ritual cave...

...If successful, one of them will become the new Black Hand.

Let me through!

send me!

Send me!!

Who said that?

The next morning.
Respen,
I'm leaving in the morning on a quest and I could not risk you talking me out of it. I may never get this chance again, and if all goes as planned, things will be very different for us. I hope to be back soon with good news.
Take care friend,
Frank

This is the ritual cave. You'll never be more thankful for your dark vision as you will inside of there.

Slek
Rugrag
the Runt
and Drobol
The four of you will enter the cave and find the Black Well.
Rugrag has been instructed on the ritual. After he performs the ritual, he will dip his hand into the Black Well and become the Black Hand.
You four must make this quest alone, but we will wait and watch for your return.

Quick! Into that small tunnel!

RAWRR!!

Oof

No!

We're safe in here but... Slek is dead. What was he thinking?! We can't fight that ogre.
You just going to give up like that?
I didn't say that.
But there might be another option. Did you see the ogres eyes? It looks like he was blinded in a fight. I think, if we go very quietly, maybe we could sneak past it.
I guess we can't stay in here forever.

Sniff
Sniff

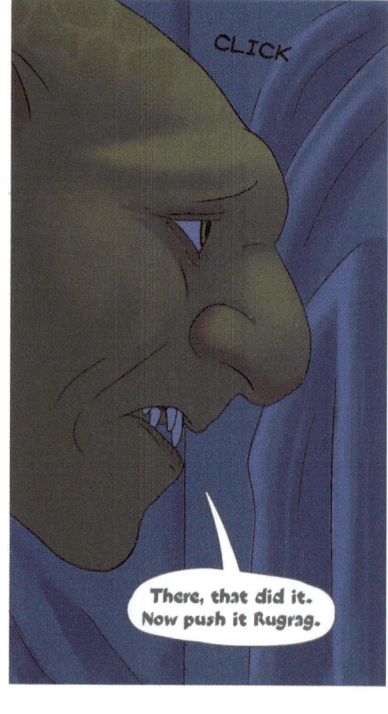

I will bathe in dwarven blood!

Here is my chance.

Die goblin filth!

uhh

RAA!

Give up, we have you! More of our brothers are arriving now.
Get the manacles ready!
Coward runt...

No... Respen...
Poke poke fun, hehe.